Faith, Hope,
and a bird
called **George**

A Spiritual Fable

MICHAEL MORWOOD

Faith, Hope, and a Bird Called George

A Spiritual Fable

TWENTY THIRD 23rd
PUBLICATIONS
www.23rdpublications.com

TWENTY-THIRD PUBLICATIONS
A Division of Bayard
One Montauk Avenue, Suite 200
New London, CT 06320
(860) 437-3012 or (800) 321-0411
www.23rdpublications.com

Cover image ©iStockphoto / sasimoto

ISBN 978-1-58595-827-6
Library of Congress Control Number: 2010942704
Printed in the U.S.A.

Contents

Prologue

My husband died fifteen years ago. Our house was too big for me on my own, so with the help of my five children I took up residence eight years later in the retirement community where I now live.

It has been a good move for me. I must say, though, that I had thought the "retirement" part would mean a far more leisurely pace of life. I have discovered it really means involvement in trips, social events, games, hobbies, and a host of other activities.

Two activities stand out for me: First, visiting speakers who expand our knowledge on a wide range of topics. Second, computer classes that have introduced me to the Internet and e-mail. What a world of learning this has opened up for me.

I found it quite extraordinary, in what I considered to be the last cycle of my life, that I was learning more about life and about the world than I could ever have imagined.

Little did I dream that four years ago, events would take my learning even further, beyond anything I might have had in mind.

In the community we have small groups in which we meet and share whatever we would like to share about life, past and present. Normally I would have no hesitation about sharing something new I had learned, but what began four years ago I have kept to myself, since no one would have believed me. In fact, my friends here would have thought I had lost my mind, because the learning came through conversations with Faith and George.

Everyone knew Faith was my cat and George my parrot.

Oh, yes, I am certain we did converse. But when you think about it, it's not so strange, is it? Many people talk to their pets and many people even think their pet is like a guardian angel or a special companion in life for them. And parrots do talk.

I named my cat Faith simply because "faith" and "hope" go together, and I've carried my name, Hope, through seventy-nine years of life.

George? Well, that's quite different. George was owned by a Catholic priest for many years. When the priest died, I was asked to care for his parrot. I named him after a clergyman I knew for many years whose name was George. That particular George was fond of quoting authoritative sources, much like a parrot, so when I received the bird to go with my cat, "George" he became.

It was Faith who started our evening conversations. Well, at least it was Faith who started to respond to me first. I should mention that I had talked to Faith and George about many things over the years, just sounding off—you know how it is when you are alone at home and you need someone to talk to, someone to listen. It was quite a shock, though, I tell you, the first time Faith answered me. I can remember the occasion very clearly. It was night time, long after I should have been in bed. I was worrying about a close friend of mine...

In the
beginning...

I had received a call early that evening from a dear lifelong friend, Jack Robinson. Jack's wife, Elsie, and I had gone to school together from kindergarten through the end of high school. I remember so fondly and vividly the excitement of the post-school years, when Elsie and I continued to share our hopes and dreams. We were probably most excited when each of us fell in love the first time… and the second…and the third. Can anything in life be more precious than having a friend with whom you can share the deepest joys and hopes and the pains of your heart? Elsie became more than a close friend. She was life companion, lifeline, anchor, inspirer, and Rock of Gibraltar all my life.

Jack called to tell me that Elsie had pancreatic cancer, and in all likelihood had twelve months or so to live.

You know in your heart these calls are going to come. You don't get to be in your late seventies without experiencing quite a number of such calls. But Elsie? And this news was so unexpected.

That's why I was up late that night, way past my usual bedtime. Memories of the joyful and tough times Elsie and I had shared captivated my attention and made the minutes and the hours speed by. All the while Faith was on my lap and I was gently stroking her. George sat silently, waiting, I guess, for me to say "good night" and put the hood over his cage.

Faith would have been accustomed to me giving voice to my thoughts as I sat with her each evening. She would have heard my reactions to news items on the television, would have been told to whom I was speaking on the telephone and what the call was about, would know what I was planning to do the next day, or what we were about to watch on television or listen to on the radio.

Nightly she would have heard me say to her and George, "OK, you two, time to close the eyes and have a good night's sleep."

This night I told her about the phone call. As we sat together in the hours that followed and I recalled life shared with Elsie, I must have muttered, "Oh, dear!" many times. Eventually my thoughts and emotions welled up into a sobbing exclamation.

"Faith, it's just not fair. I just cannot understand how such a good, loving woman who put her faith in God has to die this way. Elsie deserves better from God than this."

That's when Faith first spoke to me.

I know I was in a state of shock and distress. I also know people would have said—if I had told them—that I must be losing my mind if I really believed my cat spoke to me. However, what began that night was as amazing, and as real, and most of all, as enlightening, as any spiritual experience could be.

Faith asked, "God? Who is God?" She asked this like someone would ask, "John? Who is John?"

Trying to explain God to anyone is difficult enough, but you might imagine the degree of difficulty when your mind is reeling and you find yourself responding to your cat.

Struggling for words, I said, "God is not someone. God is, um…God is…well, God *is* someone. But God is not a human person. Um…God is like a spirit. You cannot see God. He made everything that exists."

"So what has God got to do with Elsie being sick?" asked Faith.

I was tempted to say that God is in control of everything, but something made me pause. I did not want to suggest we are just pawns in God's hands.

"Well, everything is in God's care. We call it 'providence.' It means that God is caring and knows better than we do what is good for us and that whatever happens in life is for our ultimate good."

"Even pain and sickness?" asked Faith, in a tone clearly indicating this was a bit hard to believe.

"Well, yes…it has to be, since God…um…since God permits everything to happen."

It was then that the night's second surprise was sprung on me. George spoke.

Now, George didn't hesitate the way I had. No, George stuck his chest out like he'd been waiting all his life for this moment. George had the answers.

"It's like this," he said with absolute certainty, "way, way back when God made the first humans, everything was peaceful and there was no sickness and no death. But the first humans thought they were better than God and disobeyed him, so God punished them with the loss of peace and health. Therefore sickness and death are not God's fault. They are the fault of human beings."

I was so proud of George that it overcame the wonder of hearing him speak. George had obviously heard people with some knowledge and authority speaking on this topic.

Faith, however, looked puzzled.

"George, this God character…I'm confused. Hope says he's caring and arranges everything for people's good. But you're saying he also gets upset and punishes people if they disobey him. Does God have emotions and changes of mind and mood the way Hope does?"

I didn't much like the idea of my emotional ups and downs being brought into the conversation. I guess it was not really surprising that Faith would have been acutely aware of my feelings in the preceding months as I had wrestled with getting older and less independent. But then I thought, *What a great question!* I looked to George for his response.

George looked thoughtful.

"I have heard that God can change his mind and that he certainly did so on occasions, but it seems that God does not have emotions like human beings do because God is a spirit."

That made sense to me. I have always understood that emotions are somehow linked with our human bodies and our minds. However, the very fact that it made sense raised a problem for me. I had always thought of God caring and loving like a father or mother, but also sometimes a bit angry with me. My father and mother were sometimes

annoyed with me, so I never had any trouble thinking God was like that.

"George," I said, "something is wrong here. The
Bible says God gets angry; he remembers wrongdoing; he punishes; he cares; he loves; he is disappointed when people are not faithful to what he
wants. We believe that God is like a person who
notices and hears and responds. Doesn't that mean
that God has feelings and changes in mood?"

"No. Definitely not," said George. "God is a
spirit. God does not have a body, so there are no
mood swings."

I was about to say, "But the Bible says…" and
talk about some of the passages where the Bible
makes clear that God got angry, when Faith spoke
again.

"George, I'm having trouble understanding this
person you are calling God. You said he punished
human beings with sickness and death. Hope says
something called the Bible describes God being
angry and disappointed. And you tell me this God
is not into emotion and mood changes. That doesn't

make any sense at all. And how come you know so much about him anyway?"

George took time to explain how he'd listened in on clergy conversations for many years. He clearly believed hearing the clergy talk was just one step away from hearing God talk.

"Well, if you know so much," said Faith, "tell me where this God lives."

"God does not live anywhere," said George. "I've already said that God is a spirit. God is everywhere. He holds everything in existence because he created everything that exists. Without God there can be nothing. That's why everything that happens is linked with God in some way."

"What about heaven?" I asked. "I've always believed that God lives in heaven and that when I die I will go there if I'm good enough."

"Heaven is not a place," said George. "I heard the clergy talking about a statement from the pope saying that heaven is not a place. Some clergy at this discussion said that if heaven is not a particular place where God is, then heaven must be everywhere because God is everywhere. I distinctly remember several of the clergy saying this. They said it is a mistake to think that God lives up above us somewhere."

Well, you could have knocked me off the sofa with a feather when I heard that. All my life, I thought that when I died I was going to go to some place "in the heavens" where God lived and that there would be a judgment about whether I would get in or not. George, it seems, had been listening in on clergy conversations that were not reaching the pulpit on Sundays.

"Do you mean to tell me, George, that when I die I'm not going on a journey to somewhere else where God lives?"

"That's what these men said. They seemed rather unsure of just what happens when people die and where they go, except they believed that people will meet God when they die, wherever God is."

I'd never thought of that before. I'd have to think about it a lot more. I could sense that Faith wanted to keep the conversation going, but I'd had a long, long night, and it was time for bed.

I knew I wanted to talk a lot more about God, especially whether God wanted Elsie to be sick or not. A host of other issues about God and suffering came to mind—whether God really does get angry and just where is God and...but there was only so much my aging brain could take in.

Faith and George talking to me. Imagine that!

God is everywhere.

Death is not a journey to God somewhere else.

Imagine that!

Basic questions
about "God"

The next morning was somewhat weird, to say the least. I dressed as quickly as I could manage, somewhat impatient with buttons that would not go into the right holes, and rushed, as best I could rush, to the living room. Faith was curled up on the sofa, still sound asleep. I removed the hood from George's cage and he looked at me blankly as he'd done every morning. I looked at him closely, waiting for him to say something, something profound, but no, not a word. Normally I would not disturb Faith, but I could not resist giving her a nudge, enough to make her open her eyes. She gave me that "Do not disturb" look that cats must have mastered thousands of years ago.

I spent the day looking at the two of them, waiting for someone to break the ice, but the day went by without a word from either of them. My mind was occupied with thoughts about Elsie and the idea that death might not be a journey somewhere.

I watched the evening news, then turned the set off and waited. The silence went on and on but clearly I was the only one conscious of it. Faith and George seemed oblivious to the fact that anything unusual had happened the night before. After half an hour, I'd had enough of the silence.

"Well, you two," I said, "you gave me plenty to think about. Is that it? End of conversation? Nothing more to say?" I think I was a bit annoyed at them for breaking into my thoughts the way they had—and now sitting and standing there like dumb animals.

I soon learned there was a trigger to get the conversation going. I had to initiate it—and it would happen only in the evenings, never in daytime. Sure enough, Faith gave a long stretch and George stood tall with his chest pushed out and gave me a "What do you want to know?" sort of look.

"George, you said God is everywhere, and I remember learning that as a child. But I've always thought of God as a Someone, Somewhere, Person. I like the image of God who holds me in the palm of his hand, who knows me personally and cares for me and loves me and will greet me when I die. So which is it? Is God a Someone who knows me personally or is God a vague, everywhere Presence that my mind cannot grasp?"

"Of course God knows you personally," replied George. "God is actually a Trinity of three Persons—Father, Son, and Holy Spirit—and each of those persons in the one God knows and cares for you. That is one of the foundations of Christian belief."

That reaffirmed what I had always believed, but it wasn't the end of the matter for Faith. They say cats are curious. She used her curiosity to tease out information in a way that reminded me of the story about the young Jesus quizzing the learned men in the temple.

"George," she said, "you seem to want it both ways. It sounds to me as though this Trinity you are talking about is located somewhere looking on, knowing what is happening and supposedly caring for people. Then, on the other hand, you are saying that God is everywhere. Either God is someone, somewhere, or God is an everywhere presence. So which is it?"

George's chest deflated a little, as if some wind had been knocked out of him. He looked puzzled, as if he'd never heard this discussed by the clergy, and so he didn't know quite how to answer. In replying, he spoke somewhat tentatively.

"I'm not sure. I have heard people talk about God both ways. I have also heard a lot of talk about God being a mystery that humans cannot fully understand, so I cannot give a definite answer."

Faith considered this. I kept quiet. Theology was never my strong point.

After a lengthy silence, Faith said,

"Maybe it could work like this: You say that God is whoever or whatever holds everything in existence, which suggests that God is everywhere. However, I can see that humans may find it difficult to relate to anything as vast as that. Perhaps it is easier for them to think about God more as a person, much the same way they think of themselves as persons, because this helps them to understand God as caring and loving."

"But," objected George, "humans insist that God is a person, or three persons that make up one God. They have what they call "doctrines" about this. These doctrines are like absolute truth, so many people believe absolutely that God acts the way a person does."

I wondered whether Faith would comment on the three persons in the one God, but, instead she said,

"Well, yes, they would, wouldn't they? It stands to reason that since humans think they are the smartest life form in existence—keeping the rest of us in check and bossing us around—that their idea of God would look and act much the way they do."

And after a short pause she added, "Well, that's how it sounds to me."

Silence.

During the silence, I remembered a remark I once heard—from one of my sons, I think. "If horses had gods, the gods would look and act like horses." I wanted to offer this morsel to the conversation, but I wasn't too sure that George wouldn't think I was just being silly, so I bit my tongue.

George looked as if no one had prepared him for a discussion on this topic. Faith looked very thoughtful. I sat there wondering where this was all leading and whether I'd be talking to an everywhere God or an elsewhere Person God next time I prayed.

Faith eventually jumped from the sofa and started pacing the floor. George and I watched her. Obviously something was ticking over in her mind and she was trying to get it right.

When she spoke, she was still pacing. She chose her words carefully and thoughtfully.

"This is how I am starting to understand what you are both saying. You say God is the cause and sustainer of everything that exists. You say God is everywhere. OK. So everything that exists, every-

where, is like…a way God is given expression…
or…is manifested. So the stars give God a way of
being expressed, all plants and animals give God a
way of being expressed, George does, I do…and so
do you, Hope. We all do."

George jumped in here. "Oh, you have to be very
careful saying all that. You cannot say that God is
just what we see around us."

"I'm not saying that, George. We can presume
that if God is the cause of everything, then God is
more than the sum total of what we see around us."

That's when it dawned on me that I had a very,
very smart cat. I was most impressed.

"So," Faith continued, "God is everywhere. And
everything that exists, apart from the human spe-
cies, gets on with being what they are meant to be.
They have no trouble doing that and have no problems about God, either. But human beings want to
think things out and to understand God. It helps
them to think of God in human terms they understand, as a person who loves and cares. So for
them, it is important that God be a person who can

love the way humans love. But for the rest of us, that is not an issue at all. We just get on with being what we are. So if human beings want to think of God as a person and that helps them, well and good. But from what I have heard so far, the really important point about God is that God is everywhere and everything gives God a way of coming to expression."

I was struck by those words, "everything gives God a way of coming to expression."

Me? I do that?

I had never really thought about myself that way before.

Me giving God a way of coming to expression?

Imagine that!

Prayer

I had developed the habit of going for a walk each morning in a nearby park. More and more I had found myself telling my bones to behave as I navigated the paths around the beautiful flower beds.

In the days and weeks that followed those first conversations with Faith and George, I stopped in the park more than I ever had before. Not because I was sore (which in fact I was) but because I found myself looking at—I mean looking really closely at—the flowers and the shrubs and the trees. It was as if I had discovered a new world, or that I was now looking at a previously taken-for-granted world with new appreciation. God being expressed here? In all this? And I never realized? I had spent all my years looking for God somewhere else.

What struck me was that the flowers, the shrubs, and the trees—and the lovely birds, too—had no such realization. They could not say, "God is here." I guess they had no need to.

God here?

And in me?

No wonder Jesus told people to go look at the flowers and the birds. I found myself recalling something else he said, about prayer and the need to go into a quiet place.

The park was the ideal quiet place to think about God and prayer.

I had never been much good at prayer. Most times it seemed to me that God was not listening. At least I never heard much back. One day I found myself wondering what George had picked up about prayer over the years.

I asked him that night.

The way George reacted, you'd have thought he was a high-ranking church prelate being asked to hold forth on religion. He drew himself up as tall as he could and began.

"Well, a classical description of prayer mentions raising the mind and heart to God. Humans pray because they want to honor God and thank him. They want to share their lives with God. They also seek to know what God wants them to do. Sometimes prayer involves speaking to God; sometimes it requires being still and listening to God. I've also heard that some people pray by being quiet and trying to be in touch with what is going on inside themselves, their moods, their thoughts and reactions to what is happening in life. I have certainly heard it said that there is no one way to pray."

That all made eminent sense to me. It seemed to fit with what I had heard all my life.

I sensed that Faith was not convinced by George, which struck me as strange, since surely the whole topic would have been new to her.

"George," she asked, "is God listening to all these prayers?"

"Well, humans believe that God hears their prayers."

"Does he respond?"

"Yes. I have often heard talk about prayers being answered."

"And have you heard talk about God not answering prayers?"

George reluctantly admitted that he had indeed heard talk about God not answering prayers.

"So how does God decide which prayers to answer and which prayers not to answer?"

"Oh," said George, "that is a matter of strong faith. Apparently if someone believes without any hesitation that God will answer the prayer, then the prayer will be answered."

Can you imagine what "incredulous" does to a cat's face? I can. I have seen it. Faith's eyes widened, her whiskers vibrated, and her face seemed to swell from air rushing through her open mouth.

"Oh, this is all so unbelievable! Do humans really believe that? Don't they pray for an end to war, an end to sickness, an end to suffering, an end to loneliness? Don't they pray for peace and for people to stop hurting one another? Don't they pray for a child not to die and yet the child dies anyway?

"Do you mean to tell me that people who pray for such things, who pour their hearts out to God only to find their prayers are not answered, are somehow lacking in faith?"

"I'm only saying what I've heard," said George, seeking the best escape route he could find.

Faith turned to me.

"Well, what do *you* think, Hope? You have had a lifetime of experience in this business. How does it work?"

How embarrassing to have had a lifetime "in this business," as Faith described it, and not to have a ready answer. However, I did have some tentative thoughts, following on my recent reflections in the park and at home, on God *here with me* rather than the God whom I had always imagined to be far away.

"I'm not sure, Faith. Since our conversations began, I have found myself thinking a great deal about God and where I experience God in my life. I had thought prayer was about talking to God as if God were a long way off, in heaven, and listening in the way we humans listen to one another. But I got to thinking recently: What if it is not like that? What if I really believe that God is everywhere?

"In that case, perhaps prayer is not so much a matter of sending a message out into the atmosphere to a listening God, but rather a matter of becoming aware of what I am coming to think of as a Sacred Presence all around me and within me. I find that a wonderful thought, and I'm disappointed it has taken me so many years to discover it. And since I'm new to it, I expect it will take some time to see how it affects how I pray. I will need to spend time just being aware and reminding myself quietly that God is here with me. I know I'm already looking at the world around me in a new way.

"Something else I would like to do is take some time to stop and look back over my life with this appreciation that God has been with me all my life. I may even stop imagining that God is someone who spends his time answering phone calls and deciding what to do after each call. I think I will have to let go of that idea, but it will be a big shift for me."

That was probably the longest speech I had made since my fortieth wedding anniversary celebration. I felt a release inside me, a "Wow—did I say that?" sort of experience that left a warm inner glow.

Amazing, isn't it? It took me seventy-five years to come to a sense of what prayer for me personally could be about. I was finally beginning to understand why it had taken so long. I had been trying in prayer to contact God as if God were an elsewhere reality and most of the time I sensed that either God was not listening or I was not praying properly. Now I realized it was not a matter of God listening or noticing or responding. It was I who had to listen and notice and respond—to the presence of God in me and all around me.

Imagine that!

Suffering

During my daily walks in the park, I often found myself thinking about Elsie and her illness. I recalled saying to Faith that Elsie "deserved better from God than this." I was now beginning to think of God not as a Super Being watching over us from in the sky somewhere, but as a Presence all around us holding everything together. Perhaps this way of understanding how everything is connected with God meant I would have to change my thinking about blaming God for what happened to Elsie. Perhaps God should not be thought of as an external string-puller, intervening in human affairs.

I decided to ask George what he had heard about this.

George began to explain that yes, God does intervene when he wants to and that he is caring and compassionate.

That's when I noticed the "he" language about God. Oh, I had heard people talking before about avoiding male language for God, but I had put that down as stuff and nonsense. They could not be serious, could they?

It wasn't so much the male language. It was more the realization how a lifetime of using "he" for God had led me to imagine God as a Super Person dwelling in heaven, looking down over us. I know God is not like that, so why, I wondered, would I want to keep on using language that led me to imagine God that way.

From that night on I have tried not to use "he" and "him" language when speaking about God. It seemed so strange and awkward at first, but now, several years later, the avoidance comes rather automatically.

I was lost in my distraction about language when Faith interrupted George.

"George, you are back on the idea that God is to be thought of in human terms as someone who notices and reacts, has good moods and bad moods and acts accordingly. Surely the idea that God thinks and acts this way puts severe limits on God."

"But humans are not all-powerful and all-knowing," said George.

"That's for sure," said Faith, "but your language keeps on suggesting God is a superhuman personality. He is similar to humans, only that he's bigger, better, controls the world and can do anything."

I sensed we could start going round in circles here, so I suggested we remember something else we had discussed—that God is everywhere. I ventured the opinion that if we keep this in mind, we could think that whatever happens more or less unfolds within a Sacred Presence rather than being directed from somewhere else. I was far from certain about this and what it meant. I was thinking aloud.

"Maybe," I said, "it is not a matter of a God who controls…" And then I had what I thought was a brilliant idea. "Maybe it is like gravity."

I had to give a layperson's explanation of what gravity is, and then continued. "We cannot see or touch gravity, but it is everywhere, and everything that exists in this universe operates under its influence. It does not intervene or control behavior. It just is. So maybe God could be understood as a Presence holding everything in existence, a Presence that is part of everything, and everything unfolds and continues in that Presence."

George looked decidedly skeptical. I was to discover in a later conversation why he found the notion of God as an everywhere Presence so difficult to focus on, compared to the idea of God in heaven.

"What about evil and suffering, then?" he asked. "Where does evil come from?"

I was rather sure George had an answer to his own question, the answer he had learned from years in a Catholic presbytery, an answer that put God very much in control: God is good; God made the world, therefore everything was good; the first man and woman sinned and through their disobedience suffering and evil came into the world. God punished them.

It was the same answer I had learned at school many years ago.

I knew from a lifetime of Christian living that the existence of evil and suffering is a problem for many people who believe in a good and loving God. They ask how a good God can allow suffering and evil. Some also raise the point that if God is all-knowing, then God must have known that Adam would sin, so why did God go ahead and create humanity? Surely sin has to be laid at God's door as well as Adam's and Eve's if God knew all along what was going to happen.

I knew I could no longer think about God or about the first human beings in a literal understanding of the Adam and Eve story. That understanding did not make sense. It removed God from humanity and all of creation, turned us into exiles from God, and made evil a problem that God needed to resolve instead of a reality for which we humans have to take responsibility. My newly discovered understanding that whatever God is, God is always present here in some mysterious, intangible way made more sense to me. God is not elsewhere, controlling and reacting.

I could hardly believe my audacity. Me shifting so decisively from what I had believed all my life!

The encouraging thing was that I felt a sense of freedom with this change of thinking and I wondered why it had taken so long. I realized that never before had I been exposed to a way of thinking and of seeing the world around me that focused attention on God's closeness to me. All my life I had tried to relate with a loving God, yes, but definitely a God at a distance from the likes of me.

The sense of being set free from a narrow and limiting understanding of God increased significantly in the weeks and months that followed. I discovered something of the joy that Jesus had in mind when he spoke about the woman who found the lost coin in her house. I smile now when I think of that short parable. It so aptly describes my situation. I think of the house as myself and only late in life did I find the "lost coin" that brings me so much happiness. The "lost coin" represents for me the good news of God's Presence with me.

I think there *was* a time in my life—in the freedom and the innocence of early childhood—when I had the coin. But somehow formal religion nurtured me into a story about God being elsewhere and life being an arduous journey to get to God when I die—and the coin was lost.

I now have a new appreciation of Jesus saying that unless we become like little children, we will not be able to "enter" or understand or appreciate "the kingdom of God" here with us.

But I am moving ahead…

I responded to George's question about suffering along these lines:

"I think it is true to say that evil is something only humans can do. No other life form has the capacity to do evil because it requires an act of the will, a deliberate intention to do wrong. Is that right, George?"

George nodded, so I continued.

"You cannot do evil, George, nor can Faith…"

I noticed Faith giving me a quizzical look, so I stopped to ask her what she was thinking.

"Well," she said, "I often have an intense desire to kill George and to eat him. Is that evil or not?"

George, as you can imagine, shuddered, and stepped back a pace or two on his perch.

"I've never trusted you," he said. "I've always had a sense that I should never let you come too close to me. I really don't trust cats."

"I understand, George," said Faith, "but is it evil if I want to kill you? Nothing personal about this, of course."

George thought for a while. This was hardly a topic that priests would have discussed, but I could see George was thinking hard, trying to remember information that might be pertinent to the question.

Eventually he said, "No. It cannot be evil. Hope is right. Only humans can do evil because they have a special kind of awareness as well as free will. With you and me it is a matter of instinct. Cats kill birds. Birds kill insects. It is how we learned to survive."

Faith nodded, "Almost everything that lives survives by eating something else that has lived, whether it be animal, insect, fish, plant or vegetable. A lot of killing goes on to keep everything alive, but that is not evil."

Turning to me, she said,

"So it seems, as you said, that evil is something you humans have to yourselves. If that is so, it surely has to be something that you humans can do something about. You are the ones who choose to act wrongfully."

I had to agree, as I had been thinking that way myself. I thought we needed to focus more on getting our own act together and to stop asking God to solve a problem caused by human willfulness. Prayer about evil and its harm should be directed at changing us, not about asking God to do something about it.

That still leaves suffering...

All my life I had believed that God permits suffering and gives people crosses to bear. Now I was beginning to see things differently. If I no longer thought of God as a Super Someone making decisions about who should suffer or not, then I ought not to think that God had decided Elsie should have cancer. The issue of Elsie's cancer had nothing to do with God "permitting it" or asking her to carry a cross. That image of God who intervenes and manipulates the human situation ought to be laid to rest. Or, at least, I now found myself thinking so.

Dear me, was this me thinking these thoughts?

I don't want to give the impression that my thinking about God underwent a sudden change, as if I quickly found myself standing on new ground. No, as I mentioned earlier, the change took weeks and months to settle into my mind. I should add, that while I was excited about where my conversations with Faith and George were leading me, I was also somewhat troubled by a not-so-small voice inside me saying, "How dare you think this way! Who do you think you are?" The "me" thinking these new thoughts seemed so small and inadequate when pitted against authoritative voices I had heard all my life speaking about God as if God does rule the universe and intervenes from on high.

I talked about this one evening with Faith and George.

"George, I find myself moving away from thinking about God as someone who controls the traffic, as it were. I am no longer comfortable believing in a God who decides that people like Elsie should become ill or that God permits illness for some reason. But I have a sense people might say that I'm "losing the faith" and that I cannot call myself a Christian anymore if I stop believing in a God who plans, rules, and intervenes in human lives—cancer here, a death there, blindness for him, a cure for her, success in business for this person, failure in business for that person, and so on. What do you think?"

It didn't take long to realize I'd made a mistake in asking George such an open-ended question. About an hour later, I had to intervene after he had taken Faith and me through what he called "salvation history"—an account of God having a "plan," choosing a particular group of people, making decisions, intervening, letting people know what he wanted, and finally sending "His Son" down from heaven to "save" us.

He's still holding on to that God up there directing the traffic, I thought.

"George, I've learned all that and I know it's the biblical story. But isn't there another way we could think about God and still honor the Bible?"

George looked at me blankly, as if to suggest he had certainly never heard the clergy talk about any such alternative.

Faith had listened intently to George, but whereas George did not seem able to understand why I would want to question one of the primary biblical notions of God, she seemed to appreciate what I was struggling with.

"George," she said, "Hope has been trying for some time now to think about God as an everywhere Presence rather than a heavenly ruler. It's understandable that the people who wrote the Bible thought about God the way you have just described—after all, it supported the idea that they were God's chosen people. But what if God is not really a Someone up in the heavens planning and intervening? What if, in fact, God is everywhere, as we have been discussing, and so is accessible to all people?"

"The difficulty with that thinking," said George "is that it takes away the unique role of Jesus. Christians believe that men and women only have access to God through belief in Jesus. Jesus is the unique pathway to God."

"What do you think about that?" Faith asked me.

I took some time to think about this before I responded.

"I'm not sure," I said. "I'm sensing that because my thinking about God is changing, then my thinking about Jesus may have to change also. On the one hand, I know that what George just said about God's plan and how Jesus died for the sin of Adam and Eve is what I have heard all my life. On the other hand, I have also heard all my life that Jesus told people that God was with them when they visited one another, helped one another, and cared for one another."

I paused, reflecting for a moment on my own words, and then continued,

"Strange, isn't it, that I never really believed that about myself, even though I did hear it often enough, that when I helped or cared for others God was with me."

"So Jesus was more about revealing God's presence already with people in their everyday lives rather than he was the pathway to an elsewhere God?" asked Faith.

"That's right!" I exclaimed as someone who had just been suddenly enlightened.

"From what you are saying," said Faith, "it sounds as though Jesus recognized a link between human goodness and God's presence. Perhaps he wanted people to see and believe what he saw and believed and wanted them to be encouraged by this rather than think God was a long way from them. Does that make sense?"

It certainly did to me.

I spoke slowly, trying to put my thoughts together:

"Yes, of course, Jesus revealed that God's presence was already with people! He did not bring it to them. They already had it, but they did not recognize it."

It was as if an important piece of a puzzle had fallen into place for me.

"That fits with what we have been saying about God's presence being everywhere.

"Jesus told people to open their eyes and see God's presence in their everyday lives, in their loving, and in their care for others."

I remember we sat in silence for some time as I went over in my mind what I had just said.

Eventually Faith asked, "So you have two stories in your Bible, then?"

It was more a statement than a question.

Two stories. One, about Jesus being the way to an elsewhere God. The other, about Jesus revealing God always present in everyday living.

"Yes," I responded slowly, "two stories."

"And which one gives you more dignity and hope and encouragement?" asked Faith.

I simply nodded. I had no need to put into words what had eluded me all my years as a Christian and what I was now coming to see: God is always with us. God had always been here, since the beginning of human history and before.

Faith gave me time to be with my thoughts before continuing. "So, let's go back to your original question about suffering. It seems you have two stories about God also. One story focuses on God as an Overlord and raises many difficult and unanswerable questions about how God allows or even plans suffering for people. The other story focuses on God as an everywhere Presence. It seems to me that one of the significant differences between the two ways of thinking about God has to do with whether God is an outsider in control of everything or whether God is a universal Presence.

"If you understand God to be a universal Presence, then you understand everything exists and unfolds within that Presence.

"Suffering, then, is not directed or controlled by God. Suffering is an inevitable part of existing in a universe in which change and upheavals constantly take place.

"What seems important to me on this issue of suffering is that one story puts God at a distance from you when you suffer and raises all sorts of problems about why God allows or even intends the suffering. The other story has God always close to you in the suffering and in whatever happens. That would seem to be a God worth believing in. Why would you choose not to believe this story?

"Surely your Christian religion would support you in this belief?"

Yes, I thought, surely it would.

You can imagine, though, that I had to think long and hard about all this. And it was not easy. It is not easy to question a lifetime of deeply ingrained thoughts and teachings and images about God. It is not easy to struggle with thinking that you are "losing your faith." But I decided to be gentle and patient with myself and to give myself plenty of time to reflect on the story of God always with me.

As this story about the ever-present God began to take root in the depths of my being, it released a sense of wonder and appreciation about life I had never known before.

Yes, I did eventually find the "lost coin."

In finding it, I came to wonder why and how I ever lost it.

Buried
treasure

I let several weeks go by before engaging Faith and George in conversation again. Oh, don't get me wrong, I wanted to talk about many matters, but I also felt the need for some stillness and silence. It was as if an inner voice kept inviting me, "Take time to reflect on this new sense of God with you. Become more aware of it. Look at your life and your surroundings with this awareness."

What struck me most was the thought that life with God was not so much a future reality that awaited me when my human life was finished, but something I was experiencing now, and I should try to make the most of it. It was the stunning realization that this human existence of mine was a precious and privileged experience *in* God. I had never thought of my life that way before: that being human is a way of experiencing the mystery we call God.

This was quite a shift for me. I had always thought that my life on earth was a testing ground to see if I would deserve to see God and be with God when I died. I had failed to see, or never had been helped to see, that life in or with God was already a reality. All I had to do was open my eyes and mind and heart to appreciate what it was all about.

I must admit to moments when I felt somewhat depressed. Or perhaps it was more a feeling of regret. Here, in the twilight of my life, I caught myself thinking, "It's so late in life to come to an appreciation of what life is all about. Why didn't I learn this years and years ago?"

Telling myself, "Better late than never," was not much consolation. At least, not until I realized that I could mope around feeling sad and sorry that I had missed out on the sense of God with me all throughout my life, or I could do two things. First,

I could take the time to look back over my life and see the events of my life in a new light, see God present and coming to expression in me, and see that same Divine Presence in people who came in and out of my life over the years. Second, I could live and delight in the present and face the future with the heartfelt conviction that God and I are inseparable.

I didn't think Faith and George could help me much with either of these two tasks, so I set myself a time each morning and began a routine of daily reflection on life, going back to my earliest memories, then recalling school days and slowly working through the years of my life.

What an extraordinary feast for the mind and the heart! To look back over the years and as each person and event came to mind, to hold that person or event, and to consider the sacred was *here*, God was *here*, in people who were present to me with their love, care, attention, help, teaching, friendship, or guidance. And just as I had lived all those years without putting two and two together and coming to an awareness of God in and with me, I suspect many of those wonderful people also missed seeing the connection.

Calling many people to mind and reflecting on God's presence in them worked wonders for me also. It helped me to see that I had brought something of God's presence to them.

It seems such a shame that so many of us go through life without realizing how we have touched other people with a presence that is truly sacred. What a blessing it is, then, when we take the opportunity to reflect on the reality of this, to hold it in mind and memory, and to deeply, deeply appreciate the wonder of it.

I came to discover that the more I engaged in this daily reflection, the more the practice opened me to an awareness of the now: that here and now where I am living, that here and now with family and friends, the sacred is here in our presence to one another.

Me, a sacred presence to others?

Others a sacred presence to me?

This has been true throughout my life?

Intriguing, isn't it, that we can hear words all our lives, but their meaning does not sink in? I am thinking specifically of the words somewhere in Scripture about us being "earthen vessels that hold a treasure." I spent so much effort trying to fix the cracks and the imperfections of my "earthen vessel" as if I had to put my life into almost perfect shape before God would have anything to do with me. And yet, all that time, the "treasure"—God's presence—was there! It now seems to me that it was a well-buried treasure.

So who or what buried it?

And why?

My reflections on life have provided some insights, if not answers, to these questions.

There seems to be a stage of childhood when all is well, when you are the center of the world and the world is a magical place to be explored. At least that's how it seemed to me. I saw this also in my children and see it now in their children.

Then you go to school.

At about the same time you become aware that every Sunday you are taken to a building called a "church," and learn that you belong to a group called "the Church."

I hold each of these influences, school and Church, in high esteem. I benefited greatly from both and received much for which I am deeply grateful. Yet, as I reflected on the years of childhood, I sensed these two influences in my upbringing contributed to the burying of the treasure. They took me out of a realm of innocence and connectedness with everyone and everything, even with God, and led me into a quite different world:

a world of earning praise,

a world of competing with others,

a world of comparing myself with others,

a world watched over by a God in heaven who rewarded and punished,

a world that divided people into different classes and religions and colors.

My memories of church-going as a child are filled with a sense of comfort. The word that comes to mind is "devotional." I loved the atmosphere, the sense of community, the mystery of it all, something of wonder, and the belief that this was where we made contact with God.

However, as I reflected on these years, I came to appreciate how my experience of Church also nurtured me, through teaching, story, ritual, and preaching, to believe God was basically elsewhere, in heaven, looking down on us, and that we were distant from God. I was taught that this life was a sort of trial to see whether we would get to where God lived when we died.

It did not take long in this nurturing process to learn that we could not presume to be close to God—that was only for the great saints and very holy people. No, we had to work hard to improve ourselves before God would love us more. I can see now that we were effectively immersed in an adult religious worldview—and we had best learn how things really were with us and God!

As I looked back I had a sense that something in me, something I identify with being a child—open, trusting, somehow free—had closed over during my childhood years. I realize we have to move on from being children and to take responsibility and become capable adults, but it seems to me now that my years of faithful Christian practice, so important to me, also had an unfortunate side effect. It led me to distrust my ability, my need and even my right to question what I was being taught to believe.

Amazing, isn't it, that when we became adults we could be so unquestioning about what we learned as children about God? Maybe if we had stayed "as little children" we would have asked questions!

As I observe my grandchildren these days, I am amazed at their knowledge and the way they readily ask questions. I find myself hoping that they will never stop inquiring and searching. I can see that their school education promotes the inquiry and the searching. I hope that any exposure to religious education does the same.

Imagine the end of "lost coins" and unquestioning minds and living as if God were distant from us!

Not too old
to learn

Throughout my life, most of the preaching I had listened to, the prayers we heard and read at worship, and the hymns we sang focused on Jesus as the pathway to God in heaven. He was the savior who "opened the gates of heaven for us." Why, I found myself wondering, did my religion focus so much on this role of Jesus rather than on his teaching that urged people to believe God was indeed with them, *here, now,* and to let that belief change their lives? I asked George to comment on this.

George said the focus came from Jesus' own words in John's gospel where Jesus spoke about himself as the "way" to God and that no one could have access to God except through him.

Faith looked sceptical. "He actually said that?"

"Yes. Definitely," said George. He explained what a gospel was, and added, "John's gospel is considered to be the most important of the four Christian gospels because it contains the most statements of Jesus."

"From what I have heard from you and Hope," responded Faith, "you consider Jesus to be your highest authority for speaking about God. In these gospels, did he talk about God being everywhere and accessible to everyone?"

George became thoughtful. I must admit that I did, too, as I tried to think of any statement in which Jesus proclaimed everyone had access to God.

All that came to me was the verse I knew from one of the letters of St. John, "Everyone who lives in love lives in God and God lives in them."

I mentioned this to Faith, explaining that while Jesus did not say these words, they are contained in a book of Scripture and could be understood as a sort of summary of what he preached.

"Well," said Faith, "if everyone who lives in love lives in God and God lives in them, and God is everywhere, that would seem to include people of all races and all places. Why, then, does John's gospel say that only Jesus can gain access to God?"

George gave her a "Don't ask me!" look, and two pairs of eyes then turned to me.

"I don't know!" I said with some exasperation. I wanted to tell them to ask an expert on religion, not this woman who knew next to nothing about the gospels except what she had heard in church. I had never picked up the discrepancy Faith had just pointed out. I felt some annoyance that after a lifetime of being a Christian I could not answer her.

"When was John's gospel written?" asked Faith.

George explained that scholars could not pinpoint the date, but the consensus is that it was written about the end of the first century.

That came as quite a surprise to me. I had always thought that this gospel was written by St. John the Apostle shortly after Jesus died, but it seems he was long dead before it was written.

George had to explain to Faith that humans dated years from when Jesus was born.

"And when did Jesus die?" asked Faith.

"About the year 33," said George.

"So this book was written more than sixty years after he died?"

"Yes," said George. "That may seem a long time, but Christians believe God's Spirit helped people preserve the words of Jesus through those decades before someone recorded them in writing."

"Tell me more about Jesus," asked Faith. "I recall you saying earlier, George, that God had a plan of what you called "salvation" and that God used the Jewish religion and Jesus to have this plan unfold and fulfilled. Was Jesus a Jew?"

"Yes."

"Are Jews also Christians?"

"Oh, no," said George. "Christianity is a religion completely separate from the Jewish religion."

Faith looked somewhat surprised when she heard this.

"Jesus started this new religion?" she asked.

"Yes."

"So I presume he stopped being a member of the Jewish religion if the religions are separate?"

George pondered this for a while.

"I never heard that he did," he said.

Interesting, I thought to myself. I had never heard anyone speak about that either.

"George," I said, "I have never thought about Jesus always staying within his own Jewish religion. I presumed he moved away from it when he started the Christian religion. How could he stay within his own and yet start another?"

George replied, "It seems Jesus saw the shortcomings in his Jewish religion and wanted to set it in a new direction. So he set the foundations for a new religion but never formally renounced his own."

Turning to Faith, he continued,

"Christians believe that this new religion started very early, at an event called Pentecost, just some weeks after Jesus died. It separated from the Jewish religion very early on."

Before the discussions with Faith and George had begun I would not have questioned George's statement. It was consistent with what I had been taught and had believed. Now, however, a question about something else I had heard over the years came to mind: The first followers of Jesus, even after Pentecost, went to the Temple every day to pray.

That seemed to indicate they were still associated in some way with their Jewish faith rather than being members of an entirely separate group.

And then I thought of St. Paul. I knew he preached and wrote more than twenty years after Jesus died.

"George," I asked, "What about St. Paul? Did he ever stop being a member of the Jewish religion?"

We had to explain briefly to Faith who St. Paul was, mainly in terms of his taking the message of Christianity to a wide audience.

"Well, I'm sure he died a Christian," said George.

"But is there any sign that he broke completely with his Jewish religion?" I asked.

"I don't know of any," replied George, again sounding like someone not too sure of his ground.

There was quite a puzzle here, I thought.

If Jesus and Paul and maybe all the apostles remained within their Jewish religion, then Christianity, as a religion, must have taken quite a number of years to break away from its Jewish roots. Yet I had always believed, without any reason to doubt, that, as George stated earlier, a new religion, established by Jesus, with its own rituals and beliefs quite separate from the Jewish religion, had begun at Pentecost.

Now I found myself wondering what had really happened.

A voice within me said, "Let it go. It doesn't really matter. Besides, you're out of your depth here."

However, another voice kept saying, "This is so interesting. Here's your chance to ask some of those questions you regret never asking."

Me, at this time of my life?

That's what I found truly wonderful in this upheaval about religious faith. I was curious. I was interested in learning something I had never explored. I was not too old to learn anew.

And I could do something about it.

The recent conversations with Faith and George and my weeks of reflection on losing "the lost coin" had created a resolve in me to trust the impulse to ask questions and to explore a world of ideas new to me. At long last, I was willing to take some personal, adult responsibility for my religious beliefs.

I now felt I was ready for this. Despite what many people might think about older people, I knew I was not too old to let go of beliefs that no longer had meaning for me. I was not too old to take the basics of my religious faith and expand them in a way that gave far more meaning to God and to my life. I was not too old to raise questions in order to make my faith more believable. I no longer had doubts about losing my Christian faith. If anything, my faith in God and God's presence with me had already been strengthened and broadened. I fully expected my faith would continue to be strengthened as I explored further.

I know that many people my age are sustained by a faith they have never questioned, and I believe that no one has the right to disturb their faith. But for me, and for many other people, I suspect the aging process provides a platform on which to stand and view life and beliefs in the light of personal experience. I would not have trusted my ability to do this before my conversations with Faith and George began. However, all that has happened since then has led me to appreciate there is an inner wisdom in all of us. That makes sense if we believe we give God a way of coming to expression in human form. Part of this inner wisdom is an ability to know what is really important, to know what we can let go of, and to explore our own answers about the meaning and purpose of life. We don't have to unquestioningly accept the answers packaged for us by someone else.

I decided to examine some of the packaging.

There were two issues in my mind crying out for some explanation. One, how come I'd only ever heard that the Christian religion started at

Pentecost, when the evidence seemed to suggest that the split from the Jewish religion took many years to happen? Two, how come John's gospel suggests Jesus is the unique gateway to God when Jesus himself told people God was close to them in the way they cared for one another?

It seemed to me that my lack of knowledge about the Scriptures was a factor with both issues.

I had two sources I thought might help me: the Internet and a priest, Fr. John, who regularly visits our community and is a lecturer in Scripture studies at a nearby college.

I started with the Internet.

I remembered our computer teacher showing us Wikipedia, an encyclopedia on the Internet. So I went to Wikipedia and typed in "St. Matthew's gospel," thinking I might as well start with the first book of the New Testament.

Much of what I tried to read in the Wikipedia article was beyond my comprehension, but I found these two passages helpful:

The Gospel of Matthew is closely aligned with first-century Judaism.

Most scholars believe the Gospel of Matthew was composed in the latter part of the first century by a Jewish-Christian who was a non-eyewitness whose name is unknown.

I shared these comments with Faith and George and asked George whether he had ever heard the clergy talking about any of this.

"No," said George. "I never heard much talk about who wrote this gospel or when it was written."

This comment seemed to surprise Faith.

"I'm intrigued. Hope is saying this gospel was written forty or fifty years after Jesus died. It is one of your main Christian sources. Yet it is a book written by a Jewish-Christian and apparently written for Jewish followers of Jesus. Clearly there was not a separate religion at that time, whatever you say about the event you called Pentecost, George."

Just as clearly, George did not want to pursue this topic.

"I only know and tell you what I have heard," he said. "I heard that Pentecost is considered to be when Christianity started as a new religion. I heard a lot of talk about it expanding after Pentecost. I did not hear anything about Christianity being associated with the Jewish religion for fifty years after Jesus died. If it did, it maybe was only a small part of the movement."

Faith was having none of that. "Except the links between Christianity and the Jewish religion must have been quite strong if at least one of the Christian gospels was written for a Jewish audience."

This left me wondering why someone like me can find information so readily available—and presumably fairly accurate—that is so different from the story about the Church's beginnings that George and I had heard and I had believed all my life.

Faith was also wondering. She gave voice to her thoughts, "If the break between the two religions took so long to emerge, what caused it?"

Neither George nor I had an answer for her, so the next day I went back to the Internet and typed in "Break between Christianity and Judaism." I found myself led to Wikipedia again and an article called, "Split of early Christianity and Judaism."

The things you find when you start looking!

Again, I noted some sentences from the article:

"Rather than a sudden split, there was a slowly growing chasm between Christians and Jews in the first centuries."

"It took centuries for a complete break to manifest."

"Jewish Christians, as faithful religious Jews, regarded Christianity as an affirmation of every aspect of contemporary Judaism, with the addition of one extra belief—that Jesus was the Messiah."

"The doctrines of the apostles brought the Early Church into conflict with some Jewish religious authorities, and later led to Christians' expulsion from synagogues. Early Christianity retained some of the doctrines and practices of first-century Judaism while rejecting others."

To this day, I still wonder why we were not taught this history about how Christianity developed as a religion. The history has helped me to appreciate that Jesus and Paul remained faithful to their Jewish roots to the end of their lives, while wanting people to expand their notions about God. I had always thought they had rejected their own religion.

What I had discovered led me to explore information about John's gospel.

I learned, again from Wikipedia, that this gospel was written, as George had stated, towards the end of the first century. I was especially interested to read:

The writer "seeks to strengthen their [members of the Christian community] resolution in the face of hostility and persecution from the Jewish leadership of the synagogue."

And the following:

"The discourses in John are considered by mainstream scholars to originate in homilies and sermons that are predominantly the evangelist's own composition but which expound on a saying or action of Jesus from the tradition."

I thought about that for a long while, but didn't really understand what it was suggesting. That's when I summoned up the courage to ask Fr. John if he would call in one day and help me with some information.

I guess the last thing he was expecting on arrival was a conversation about John's gospel. Naturally I could not tell him what had sparked my interest, but he readily understood and appreciated the "how come" nature of the issue for me. I explained that I had tried to resolve the question for myself but the language of Wikipedia was beyond me. I wasn't even sure what the "discourses" were. And I was not sure whether the articles I had read in Wikipedia were accurate. He assured me, however, when I shared what I had learned from Wikipedia about Matthew's and John's gospels, that this reflected the views of many Scripture scholars.

I could write pages and pages about the conversation I had with him. He was so clear and patient.

I marveled at the way he put things in a way I could understand. I should add that at the end of our meeting I prevailed on him to be one of our visiting speakers. He came and gave a most enlightening talk on what the major religions have in common—and was enthusiastically invited to return.

I'll share just some of his comments that helped me understand why John's gospel has its particular emphasis on Jesus.

He explained that the "discourses" in the gospel are long speeches of Jesus, but that these speeches would not have been spoken as such by Jesus. They are, as the Wikipedia article says, the writer's "own composition" developing his understanding of Jesus and his role.

"Do you mean the writer just made it up?" I asked.

"Oh, no," Fr. John replied, "the gospels were all written under the influence of God's Spirit present and working within a community. All the gospels were written in the light of years of reflection on Jesus and what was happening in a particular community. That is why the gospels are different from one another— they each reflect the concerns of the community in which they were written. The community for which John's gospel was written, as you have noted from the Wikipedia article, faced opposition and needed to be clear in its understanding of Jesus in the face of Jewish criticism.

"The gospel's understanding focused on Jesus having a unique relationship with God, beyond being a prophet within the Jewish tradition. So, no, this is not something "just made up." This belief about Jesus arose from many years of reflection on his preaching and his resurrection."

"What about the saying that no one can come to God except through Jesus?" I asked. "That seems to contradict Jesus' own insight and preaching about God being close to people."

Father John picked his words very carefully in responding.

"In the face of what was almost certainly very strong opposition, the community of John's gospel asserted it had claim to something, through Jesus, that its critics did not have—access to God, or God's Spirit. This gospel is very focused on Jesus and his role in achieving a special relationship with God. The other, earlier gospels, focus more on Jesus' message.

"If we appreciate the background for each of the gospels we will avoid pitting the message in one gospel against what is found in another. No one should say the understanding of Jesus in John's gospel is right and the preaching of Jesus or the understanding of Jesus in another gospel is wrong. All understandings and approaches are important to the Christian community. The heart of the collective gospel message is: Jesus revealed God's presence with all people; Jesus is unique in his relationship with God."

"So," I asked, "it would be wrong just to pick out that statement about Jesus being the only way to God and say everyone has to believe it?"

"The Christian religion has put a lot of investment in that statement and used it to support Christianity's unique identity," he responded.

"I'd be more inclined to urge people to understand the situation from which the statement emerged. That might help them not to be so black and white about using it as proof, as some people use it, that only Jesus can access God or to show that God lives only in heaven."

"But what about the Our Father?" I asked. "Jesus prayed to God in heaven, didn't he?"

"Well, no, he didn't," Fr. John said with some conviction. "In Aramaic, Jesus' own language, 'heaven' was understood as everywhere. Heaven embraced the whole universe, and God's presence was like the breath or the wind or the spirit all through the universe. When Jesus spoke about the 'kingdom of God,' he was urging people to become aware of the breath of God always with them and to give witness to it.

"However, when Jesus' words were translated into the Greek language, the image changed because the Greeks imagined heaven as a place up above them."

Recalling conversations with Faith and George, I asked, "Where do you think heaven is?"

"Ah, the history about this is fascinating. There was a huge difference between what the great Christian thinkers thought and wrote, on the one hand, and what ordinary Christians imagined, understood, and were exposed to in their liturgies, on the other. Many, if not most, of the great thinkers who shaped Christian doctrine and the Creed in the first five centuries focused on Jesus winning access to God in heaven and on who Jesus had to be in order to achieve this. They consistently thought of heaven in the Greek imagery, as a place above the earth. It is from this thinking and imagery that Christians acquired the imagination and belief that God is really in heaven and that this life is a preparation for being with God in "the next life." This thinking suited the Christian religion well because it could claim, and did claim for many centuries, that only Christians could get to heaven.

"While all this great thinking was going on in the first five centuries, Christian art, prayer, worship, and sacramental practice took a completely different direction. They did not concern themselves with an afterlife or with God being somewhere else. They focused on *this life*. In practice, Christians gathered in the belief that God was there with them. The image of 'paradise' was frequently used to promote understanding that Jesus had regained what was lost through Adam's sin. The belief was that if paradise had been regained through membership in the Church, then Christians should give witness to God's presence with them. It was quite a wonderful vision of life and it set high ideals for people to achieve in terms of justice, generosity, and works of mercy.

"In those early centuries, baptism focused on entrance into and commitment to this "new life." The Eucharist ritualized that the people gave their Yes to being the Sacred Presence in the world. It was all very, very affirming and challenging."

With a smile, he added, "Jesus would have been more at home with these people, I think, than with those who argued over how he gained access to God in heaven.

"So where do I think heaven is? I think those early Christians in the pews were right. They learned from Jesus that we should live as if God's presence is here with us and we should make that presence clear in all we do. So I think heaven is all around us. It's just that in our human mode of existence we have a very limited perception of it."

It was only some time later that I would come to appreciate this final comment by Fr. John.

In the meantime I was thankful for his patient explanations. One thing he did urge me to do and which I have found quite helpful, is to read John's gospel in the way I might read poetry—not to get stuck on words and literal meanings but to allow the words to float in my mind and expand my understanding that all is "one" in God.

I asked him to suggest some books about the gospels, written for people without an academic background. I was delighted he was able to suggest several that I did buy and could understand.

Me reading books about how the gospels were written!

Hard for my children and friends to imagine that!

Giving **meaning** to life

As if I did not have enough to think about, two months after I had met with Fr. John one of the visiting speakers here gave a talk on the importance of giving meaning to life.

I had never seriously thought about the topic before. I had taken for granted what my religion had taught me: This life was a preparation for the "next life" with God in heaven. Now I had found myself questioning the idea that God was somewhere in the heavens waiting for me to come to him—and whether God was a "him" at all.

Following the talk, I realized the meaning of life for me would have to be shaped in a different understanding—that this life and God's presence are intertwined. Since I had come to this new appreciation of God's presence with me through the conversations with Faith and George, I decided to explore life and its meaning with them.

I wasn't quite sure how to raise the topic but one night I found myself asking them,

"What do you think life is all about?"

"What do you mean?" asked Faith as if the question were utterly meaningless to her.

"Well, why do we exist? Why do we have life? What is the purpose of life?"

Faith looked blankly at me. This was clearly some human nonsense.

"I live to be a cat. What would you expect me to say?"

I must admit her answer sounded obvious enough but somehow I had expected more.

Faith saw my look.

"What? Is that not enough, that I be what I am—a cat—and I try to be good at it?"

It sounded so simple. To be good at what I am. I liked that.

"What about you, George?" I asked.

"Same as Faith," he replied, "only I happen to be a parrot and I like being what I am."

Because George usually liked to talk on and on about everything, I was surprised by the brevity of his reply. I waited for him to say more, but nothing came.

The silence had an air about it, as if the two of them were leaving the space for me to enter, wanting to hear why this was even a question for me.

I didn't say anything. I was going over Faith's words in my mind, pondering *being good at what I am*.

The silence lingered.

Eventually, Faith looked up at me from my lap and asked,

"Well, how would you answer the question?"

"I'm thinking about what you just said. It seems to be easy enough for you and George. You are what you are and you clearly are contented with that. But it's different, I think, for us humans. I heard a talk recently on giving meaning to life, and in our group discussion after the talk we covered many topics…what value life has, how we compare with others, what we have achieved, how we have related with other people, how we relate with God, whether there is life after this life, have we acted the way our religion or society wants us to, what level of suffering we have experienced, and…oh, the list goes on and on."

Faith and George looked at me as if they could not believe what they were hearing. If birds and cats could express pity, this would have been as close as you could get.

I quickly concluded I was on my own with this topic.

"I'll think about this some more," I said to them.

In the weeks that followed, I took time to consider my life and its meaning. I saw that I would answer questions about the meaning of life quite differently at various stages of my life, from when I was newly married, for example, to when my last child left home or to when I became a widow.

Our lives take us down many roads. New issues, tasks, responsibilities, events, and questions emerge that we try to make sense of, but usually not in ways that preoccupy us. Well, that's the way it was for me. Life just went on and I tried to make the best of it. I never spent much time trying to uncover a deeper meaning in whatever was happening.

But now I wanted to give the meaning of life serious consideration.

I was exceedingly grateful for the opportunities to be quiet and reflective, to sit with my memories and let the movie of my life unroll.

I looked for significant threads that could help me find meaning and tie the stages of my life together.

One thread that loomed large was the fact that throughout life I have been loved and accepted for who I am and that I have been able to love in return. That may sound trite, but it captures something of the moments in life when I would stop in wonder and gratitude for being loved. I guess we have all had those moments when we cherished the wonder of love. I know I was often struck by the mystery: Of all the men and women in the world, how come my husband and I met and loved as if we were made for each other? How come I was blessed with wonderful friends like Elsie who accepted me as I am?

I never took love for granted, but I had never stopped long enough to see just how much of my life was threaded through with love. As I reflected, it became more and more clear to me that love and friendship have defined a pattern of life for me, have enriched my life and made it worthwhile. How fortunate I have been!

Another defining thread in my life has been my religious faith. It provided a set of beliefs and values and guidelines which gave me a sense of security and direction. Even now, as I find myself questioning some of the beliefs, my religious faith still grounds me and is very important to me. I must add also the wonderful sense of belonging and support that my church community provided.

I regretted I couldn't really converse with Faith and George about any of this. But, on the other hand, these reflections brought home to me something of the uniqueness of being human.

I have continued this practice of reflecting on life. As I have done so over these past several years, some pieces of life's puzzle have come together in a way that makes sense for me. Those pieces are God, me, love, other people, and how everything is connected. I have discovered a new and wonderful way to reflect on my life, becoming more aware and more appreciative of Hope in the world around her, Hope in her loving relationships, Hope in relationship with the mystery of God, Hope growing older, and Hope living with the mystery of what follows death.

The clearest, strongest realization I have come to from my reflections is that I have had seventy-nine years of giving expression to God in human form.

To be what I am—and to do it the best I can. How grateful I am to Faith for her words. To give God the best possible human expression I can. I now consider that to be the heart and soul of everything. It's the thread that now ties everything in my life together. This life of mine has been a journey *in* and *with* God. I am so delighted that this understanding has finally dawned! It has given me the best possible explanation for my life and its meaning.

I once heard a Catholic priest urge the congregation "to be on earth the heart of God." At the time I thought it was quite a presumptuous undertaking.

Now it makes sense to me.

Me, Hope, to be on earth the heart of God?

Me, Hope, to live life in that belief and to make it evident in all I do?

Imagine that!

How wonderful!

Bringing more **threads together**

A year or so before I came to this retirement community my youngest daughter, Helen, discussed with me a talk she had attended at her church. The people present at the talk were invited to rate themselves on a scale of one to ten on how close to God they considered themselves to be. Helen asked me how I would score myself. I remember saying that I could not presume to give myself a high score and I chose five. Naturally I was interested to hear the score she had given herself. She had also given herself five.

"But now," she said, "I would score ten."

That really caught my attention.

I asked her what had happened to make her change her mind so dramatically.

She said that after people had rated themselves, they were arranged into groups to share why they had given themselves whatever score they had decided on. Why, for example, seven and not nine? Why four rather than six? After this sharing, the presenter indicated that, in his experience, most Christians tend to give themselves a low rating. He then invited the groups to explore what they considered closeness to God depended on. Helen said her group mentioned factors such as how often people prayed, how kind they were, whether they were selfish or not, were they good parents, and a host of other items.

Helen found the open session that followed the group discussion most revealing. The presenter suggested that God was always close with everyone, and in fact, could not be any closer, ever. The issue is not a matter of people doing things to get closer to God. It is about awareness of God's pres-

ence always with them. He said it might be correct
to score low if people were scoring their *awareness
of or conviction* about God's presence with them,
but never for God's presence. He made the point
that we could not exist without God being always
present to us. The presence is always ten out of ten
whether we are aware of it or believe it or not.

He believed that one of Christianity's biggest
mistakes has been to lead people into thinking they
are somehow distant from God.

Helen related how the speaker used the scoring
exercise to talk about the purpose of prayer and
worship. Their true purpose, he said, is to deepen
awareness of God always with us and to challenge
us to give witness to God's presence with us in the
way we live.

So, by the end of the evening, Helen, realizing that
God's presence with her did not depend on anything
she did, thought she could change her score to ten.

"It seemed so presumptuous at first, to do that,"
she told me, "but really, it is just recognizing that
God is close to me. And I can see now that the chal-

lenge for me is to heighten my awareness of God's presence with me and to show it by the way I live.

I remember so clearly Helen sharing this with me and being excited by it. Naturally she wanted me to jump my score up to ten also, but old habits and old beliefs die hard, don't they? I heard what she was saying but I think I mentally upped my score to about seven—not daring to fully believe what I had heard—and continued as I was.

That was about nine years ago. At the time Helen was very active in the church community. Now she doesn't go to church at all. The strange thing is, I would say she is more religious and more spiritual now. She is more interested in learning about religion and spirituality and is constantly reading about the history of Christianity, attending seminars and workshops on spirituality, and praying with various groups. Occasionally she tried to share with me some of what she has learned, but I think she suspected all along that I was beyond changing my mind-set when it comes to religious beliefs.

Well, she was right about that.

But after almost a year of discussions with Faith and George and after my session with Fr. John, I was yearning to hear more from Helen without letting her know about my nightly conversations and how my religious thinking had been turned upside down. I hoped she might help me pull some threads together. I also relished the idea of bonding with my daughter at a new and deeper level.

So when Helen offered to drive me 240 miles to visit a brother of mine in a nursing home, I seized the opportunity to sound her out.

I started innocently enough. "Do you remember telling me some years ago that we should score ourselves ten out of ten for being close to God?"

"Sure," she said. "I don't think you ever really believed it, though."

"Well, it might come as a big surprise to you, but I do now. I'm a slow learner, I guess. I suppose you still believe it?"

"Definitely. We can never be cut off from God. We can only fail to be aware or refuse to believe that God is with us."

"How do you think of God?" I asked.

"Oh, that has changed quite a lot over the years. I think of God as a mysterious presence all throughout the universe and beyond. It fits with the ten out of ten."

She smiled. "There is no escaping the closeness of God."

I couldn't resist asking her, "I know you no longer go to church. Do you still consider yourself to be a Christian?"

She took no offense at the question.

"Ah, Mom, I'll always be a Christian. I just don't accept theology based on the claim of exclusive access to God or any claim to have certainty about what God thinks on important matters. I long to see the day when Christianity and all other religions get together and proclaim that God is accessible to all people regardless of their religion."

I wondered aloud whether that would just make one religion as good as any other.

"No," she said, "there will always be a place for different religions. Each will have its own insights about the mystery of God and how people might live in relationship with God. But religions need to stop making claims about exclusive access to God. God is accessible to all people."

"So what is special about Christianity?" I asked. She did not hesitate.

"In a word, Jesus. However, I believe Christianity has to refocus on Jesus' preaching rather than on its own theology about Jesus winning access to God in heaven as if God had been separated from humanity."

She paused, doubtless aware that this was a big topic and probably also wondering whether she was wasting her time expounding on it with me.

I asked her to tell me more about refocusing on Jesus' preaching.

I was glad we had plenty of open road ahead of us and she was able to relax and settle into a topic she was obviously at home with and keen to talk about.

"The heart of Jesus' message was what he called 'the kingdom of God.' He did not tell people God was far away. Rather he told them that God could be experienced in their everyday living, when they looked after one another, when they were ready to forgive and so on. He wanted the awareness of God's presence with them to transform the way they interacted. He wanted people to be neighborly, to act compassionately, to care for the poor, to put an end to violence. He longed to see an end to the domineering political, military, and religious powers of his day that suppressed people into fearful submission. He believed that if the human community could be empowered by a sense of close connection with God, people would establish a social system much better than what was on offer at the time."

She paused, then added, "It all has to do with justice, compassion, and a better world for everyone."

"So it is not surprising that the people with power wanted to kill him?" I asked. "He was upsetting the apple cart."

"Right. They wanted to kill the message, not only Jesus. The message was too threatening to people with power."

She paused again.

"Christianity has made such a mistake in focusing on the death of Jesus as a price to be paid for human sin and for gaining access to a distant God in heaven. He was killed because his message was too dangerous. It gave ordinary people hope that they could accomplish great things and change society for the better."

She drove several miles in silence. She seemed sad, so I remarked on it.

"Oh, yes, it saddens me, all right. I think of Jesus trying to empower people into action with a vision about God's closeness to them —and ready to die for what he believed and preached. Then I think of my years in a Church that rarely preached to me what Jesus really preached, never challenged me to stand up and be counted, knowing God is at my side. It was as if the Church never expected much of me except to keep the rules and not to ask questions. Isn't that reason to be sad when you think of what Jesus wanted?"

Yes, I thought, it is reason to be sad.

On the other hand, I couldn't help thinking of the huge number of Christians who would say that their Church experience had been positive. And it is obvious that the Church has promoted and produced extraordinary generosity and heroic service in the name of Jesus and in the belief that God's Spirit is present and active in its members.

I mentioned this to Helen.

"Yes. That is true and my life has been touched and enriched by such people. I am not calling into question that the Church produces amazing people. I just think it could proclaim its message far more effectively and stop the bleeding that is going on today."

"The bleeding?" I asked.

"Yes. Look at the exodus from the Church by people my age. And it's not just my age group. Look at your grandchildren and the young. Maybe, your own age group. Isn't the Church all round losing large numbers?"

I had to admit that was so. I asked what she thought the cause was.

"I think," she said, "people leave the Church for many different reasons, too many for me to list. However, I suspect that at the heart of many of the reasons or causes is lack of affirmation. People feel that their own life experience is not trusted or valued. I think that has something to do with Church leadership generally being too remote from people, so it talks down to them. Or it protects the institution at all costs. If the Church proclaimed Jesus' insight into who we are and what we are challenged to do, and did this at all levels of society and at all levels of the Church, I'd be back in the pews tomorrow. There's the problem—and the solution."

We talked a lot more on the journey there and back. Helen quickly caught on to the change in my thinking and was delighted to converse with me. Naturally she wondered, and asked, what had led to the change in me. I put it down to hearing Fr. John preach, talking to him and to some reading he suggested.

"Faith, Hope, George, Father John, and a journey with Helen." No, tempting as it might be, that would

be too long a title for this book. But I do want to put this journey and the talk with Helen alongside the other conversations.

I am grateful for her words about Jesus and his preaching that God is accessible to all, and for hearing that Jesus wanted to "empower" people. That word, "empower" made a deep impression on me.

Even more, I am grateful for a daughter and for my other children who each reveal that the message of Jesus is alive in them by the way they live.

Beyond **this life**

I had been expecting the call.

Bill phoned to say Elsie had died peacefully, surrounded by her family.

I had thought I might be grief-stricken on hearing the inevitable news, but that was not so. I think not wanting Elsie to suffer and knowing that death was a release for her helped me cope with losing my dearest friend.

What surprised me was the question I found myself asking: "Where is Elsie now?" Naturally enough, this led me to reflect on what awaits me at some time in the future. What is beyond the grave? Will I be conscious of being who I am in some new "spirit form" when this body of mine finally gives up on me? What about heaven and judgment and meeting God, and all the images and notions about this that I have carried most of my life?

Death gives us plenty to think about, doesn't it?

I found myself also wondering about Faith and George. Did they think about death?

I asked them what death meant for them.

"Death," said Faith, "is not something we cats think about, at least not our own dying. That seems to require some ability beyond our capacity—to think ahead and to weigh up ifs and buts and possibilities and unknowns. I'm thankful we cannot do it. It saves us a lot of anxiety. That's probably why we make such good companions for you humans. We live in the present and enjoy the now as best we can. If we thought about death we might be as neurotic and anxious as some humans seem to be."

I wondered whether Faith was having a go at me there. After all, she didn't know too many humans.

I decided not to pursue that line of thinking with her. It made me think, though, how religious ideas about dying and meeting a judgmental God do indeed cause anxiety in many religious people.

"What about you, George? You must have heard quite a number of conversations about death. What did you hear?"

"I heard more about funerals than about death as such," said George. "There are significant differences in the way clergy handle funerals. I guess that is connected with how they understand what happens at death. Some clergy treat all funerals, not only the tragic ones, as somber occasions. They talk a lot about people being judged and their wrongdoing being revealed and the need to be cleansed somehow before life with God in heaven is possible. Other clergy seem to presume life with God is almost automatic at death and focus on celebrating both the dead person's life and the beginning of what they call 'new life' with God.

"As I said in an earlier conversation, some doubt there is a 'place' to which people go when they die, but they all seem to believe that whatever lives on after death leaves earth."

"Why would they do that?" asked Faith.

Good question, I thought. Back to you, George.

George gave the answer I should have been able to give.

"I think it is because of the stories in the gospels about Jesus going up into heaven after he died. Most of the talk I heard about this suggested that Jesus went up somewhere and met God there. Christians believe that what he did made it possible for them to go where he went when they die."

Yes, I thought to myself, I carried that belief and the images that go with it all my life.

"Oh, dear," said Faith, "human imagination!"

"That sounds too dismissive, Faith." I ventured to say. "You said you had no capacity for thinking about this sort of thing, so it seems unfair for you to chide humans for doing the best they can to think about the mystery of what happens when we die."

Faith was not at all deterred by my comment.

"I said I did not spend time thinking about death as a future personal reality. But we cats—and I suspect this would be true for many animals—know what death is. Some of us can sense it in the air. Now, how can we do that? I may not have your human capacity for thinking about the future, but I do have an acute sense that everything is somehow connected with everything else. And I have a sense that here, and I mean, *here*, is where everything happens. Have we not been saying precisely this about your idea of God—that God really is *here?*"

I had to nod in agreement. She continued,

"If God is everywhere, then everywhere includes *here*, doesn't it? So I'm puzzled to hear that you humans imagine you leave earth and go *somewhere else* when you die."

George had trouble with this. It clearly did not fit with all that he had heard.

"But, Faith, you cannot say the gospels are wrong about what happened to Jesus when he died!"

"It depends on what you think is wrong," she replied. "Wrong about what happened to Jesus when he died, no. He met God and continues to exist in God. Wrong imagination about how something happened, yes."

She went on. "I have no idea how Jesus met God. I have no comprehension of what God is or is like, but I do question any imagination suggesting death took Jesus on a journey up into the heavens, beyond earth somewhere, and that is where the encounter with God took place."

Now, isn't that something, I thought. A cat disputing how humans imagine what happens after death!

She'd made me think, though, and I thought more about it as I pondered the question that sparked the conversation: Where is Elsie now?

It is comforting to think that Elsie is in heaven with Jesus and God. What could be more wonderful, rewarding, and fulfilling than that? Why would I want to question it?

The following day, I came to see that being with God in a way that is "wonderful, rewarding, and fulfilling" was not what I was struggling with. I firmly believed that. Death is not the end of us. I believed and still believe that something beyond anything we can imagine happens when we die. And I believe whatever happens hinges on a continuing relationship with God.

It was not the *with* God aspect causing my struggle. It was the *where*. Faith's comments had led me to focus on the *here, with* God, rather than a journey *to* God, out there somewhere.

Does it really matter, I found myself wondering, that I don't know what happens in death and don't know where Elsie is now. If the end result is being with God and Elsie is happy and one day I'll be eternally happy also, why bother trying to get clear answers to questions that seem to have no clear answers anyway?

I spoke to Faith about it again the next night. I tried to explain that human language about going to God in heaven when we die is just a human way of trying to explain a mystery.

Faith rolled her eyes as if to suggest she was being asked to believe the unbelievable and would have to be very patient with someone so naïve.

"My concern," she said, "is the way you humans want to separate yourselves from the natural world around you. You are a strange lot! You say God is here with you but when you talk about what happens when you die, you talk about going to some-where outside this world as if God is there and not everywhere."

"Well, yes, that is what many people imagine," I admitted.

"And when you think like that," said Faith, "you disconnect yourselves from everything around you, as if God is not really here."

She paused to let that sink in, then continued,

"And another thing, it seems to me that only humans and your God are there, in this 'heaven' where you imagine you go. Your God seems to like staying home and being preoccupied with humans."

Catty. That's what I thought.

Catty.

Envious? Jealous?

Or maybe Faith was hitting a nerve and I didn't like it.

"Faith, you're being a bit hard on humans."

"I don't think so," she replied. "Consider this: You humans seem intent on speaking for yourselves only. Who speaks for the rest of the universe where you say God is present? Who reminds you— as you seemingly need to be reminded—that the universe and the world around you produced you? Look at the cycles of life and where things come from. You say that your God is present and active in all this, and then you want to divorce yourselves from it all when you die as if all this, the universe and this planet, are not where your God is. I just don't understand how you can think that way."

"So what are you suggesting?" I asked.

"I don't have any clear answer. But I have two suggestions. First, think of death more as a change, a transformation, from the human way of living with God into some other way of living on with God—but it is not elsewhere, in some faraway place. Second, focus more on *here,* on the natural cycles of life and death, on how everything works and is connected, and on God being here in it all. Do this when you think about where you, and all of us, come from. Do it also when you think about what is beyond death."

I could see Faith was challenging me to stop thinking as if the earth had been set up as a temporary home for humans until we went to where life really began—with God in heaven.

"I like your challenge to take seriously God-here and to think about life and whatever is beyond death in that light," I said.

I thought to myself…maybe "heaven" is really here, everywhere…now. What a way to think about everything!

That's when I came to appreciate Fr. John's final comments to me about Jesus.

Light dawned.

Oh, that is just how Jesus did think!

That is what he wanted people to understand. God's presence, "heaven" is here. Act as if this were so.

What a wonderful vision of human life!

"God, here, all around us…" I mused aloud. "That would also make our deceased family members and friends closer to us than we have ever imagined."

I paused, thinking this over. "And when we die,

it would make us closer to our loved ones still here than we could ever imagine."

"Yes," said Faith, "and just as significant, it is a way to think about everything being in ongoing communion with God and with everything else that exists. We are all in this together, in the constant cycle of death and new beginnings."

"I thought you said you were not much good at abstract thinking," I said with considerable wonder and admiration.

"Yes, but with this issue something clicked inside for me and away I went!"

"I like what you said about speaking for the universe. Maybe that's what clicked?"

"I have no idea where it came from," said Faith. "It's as though some sort of energy or presence inside me took over."

"I'm grateful for whatever it was," I said. "Your comments will make me pause and consider that we humans are not the only voice of the universe and the world around us. We have a lot of listening to do."

"Imagine that!" exclaimed Faith.

A **farewell**

You get to attend quite a number of funerals by the time you reach your late seventies. I wanted Elsie's funeral to be a celebration of a life well lived and of a release into a whole new life with God—however and wherever that happens. With all that had been going through my mind in the months prior to her death, I hoped the priest would not dwell on judgment and meeting God in heaven somewhere.

I need not have worried. The service exceeded my hopes and expectations.

I was delighted to hear the priest ask the question of us: "What did you learn about God from knowing Elsie?"

Now, that was new. I had never encountered this focus at a funeral before.

What made it even better was that the priest invited us to spend a minute or so in silence, to think how we would respond to the question.

The priest had known Elsie for many years. He said that just as we look at Jesus and ask what we learn about God from contemplating his life and teaching, so we could look at the life of anyone who lives lovingly and see in their loving the presence of God with us, because living in love and living in God are so intertwined.

He had a wonderful way of talking about what Elsie did and who she was for people. Several times he stopped and said, "And here, God was with us."

One of the readings was particularly meaningful for me. It resonated so well with the discussions that Faith, George, and I had shared on God's presence and on death:

Reading

We believe we exist in God, a God beyond our images and descriptions, a God beyond the many names we use: Universal Mind,

Breath of Life, Creator, Source, and Sustainer of everything that exists.

Everywhere we look, this Energizing Presence comes to visible expression. We believe that each of us gives this Presence and Source a unique way of doing so.

Everywhere we look, we can observe the perpetual rhythm of new life, followed by death, followed by new life. So we do not believe that death is the final end of anything, nor is it for us the start of a journey to somewhere else.

Rather, it is a transformation and a continuation of the ebb and flow of existence in ways we do not understand.

Elsie's death speaks to us of the wonder of being human in a universe so vast and so magnificent and of our existence within a mystery and a power that we cannot understand or put into words.

In a very real sense, this vast and magnificent universe of ours came alive and became aware in Elsie. She gave God a way

*of coming to expression, here in our lives,
here in a way that reached out and touched
us, as daughter, wife, mother, grandmother,
sister, relation, or loyal friend.*

*She lived and loved in God, God lived
and loved in her, and in death she lives on
in God.*

The Prayers of Thanks that followed the readings
gave me great joy.

Joy? At a funeral? Yes, because the prayers em-
phasized how Elsie had given God a way of coming
to expression.

It was wonderful to hear the large congregation
strongly affirming the beautiful spirit of the woman
who had loved and been loved so dearly.

We were invited to read the responses, here in
italics.

Prayers of thanks

We give thanks for the many ways Elsie's
life touched ours.

We give thanks for the generosity of her loving...**R.** *an outpouring of God's love in human form.*

We give thanks for her faithfulness...**R.** *a mirror to us of God's constant presence with us.*

We give thanks for her laughter and sense of fun and delight in life...**R.** *the Breath of Life moved freely in her.*

We give thanks for the ways Elsie mothered, nurtured, encouraged, and supported...**R.** *truly, God was here among us.*

We give thanks for the courage with which she faced illness and death...**R.** *the human spirit has extraordinary depth to it.*

In the weeks after the funeral I reflected a lot on those last two responses: *God, here among us* and *the human spirit has extraordinary depth to it.*

Throughout my life I have come across people of amazing courage. With some people you expect it, but what has struck me is how often I have seen this courage where I never expected it. My husband was a real wimp when it came to sickness, so the way he faced cancer and the reality of death was a total surprise to me. His dying made me more aware of the courage and the depth of the human spirit. I saw the same depth again in a young nephew in his early thirties as he confronted death, in a young couple who lost their first child in a tragic accident, and in my sister who endured a long illness before she died. I have seen it in many people. However, it was only in the weeks and months following Elsie's death that I came to appreciate more deeply the connections among human spirit, spirit of life, and spirit of God.

There is a lot more to being human than I ever realized.

My other lasting impression of Elsie's funeral was the reflection one of her grandsons read at the crematorium. I like the way it acknowledged, yes, Elsie has gone, but just as surely, she is still here with us some way.

I have a strong sense of that.

Reflection: *Where Am I Now?*

Do you know that every atom
*   in my body, here before you,*
was manufactured in a massive explosion
*   in a star billions of years ago?*

Do you believe, as I do,
in a Spirit of Life at work
*   for billions of years*
that finally brought human form
*   to those atoms?*

In me the Spirit of Life and Love
came to visible expression in human form
*   when I loved you,*
*   when I called you my friends,*
*   when I laughed,*
*   when I cried,*
*   when I did whatever you loved about me.*

Where am I now?
I continue to dance
with the Spirit of Life and Love
*   in ways beyond words and images.*

But I am with you,
   and always will be
as this Spirit continues to move
   in your lives.

I am with you,
   and always will be,
in the Spirit of Life and Love.

In the days after the funeral, the priest's question about what we learned about God from knowing Elsie became an abiding thought. It was not just Elsie I was thinking about. I was thinking also of myself. How might people answer such a question about me?

What a challenging question!

My initial reaction was to shrink from the question, but I reminded myself about being "on earth the heart of God." I had accepted that this was not a presumptuous thought. I had thought of Elsie being on earth the heart of God. I readily accepted that. So, I said to myself, think about it. What personal qualities would I name?

It is perhaps not surprising that something wonderful happened. I named some qualities and said to myself, yes, Hope, this is God coming to expression in you.

What a wonderful thought that was. It's a thought that continues to delight me every day.

Perhaps at my funeral, friends and family members will speak about me this way if they are given the opportunity?

Imagine that!

Trusting life

Five weeks after Elsie's funeral, Faith died. There was no warning, there were no good-byes. I thought she was still sleeping when I went into the kitchen in the morning, so I bypassed her and went to George. George looked unwell, as if all his vitality had vanished. I fussed over him for some time and then decided to take him to the vet, since he was not responding to anything I offered. That's when I went to wake Faith...

I think I cried as much that morning as when my husband died. It was not just the suddenness, the sense of something being wrenched from me that upset me. It was the sheer loneliness that hit me. With other deaths or tragedies, we can talk about it and share our loss with family and friends, but Faith…I could tell no one what Faith really meant to me.

I realized that George knew before I did that Faith had died. Like me, he was heartbroken.

He never spoke again, never recovered.

He died three days later when I left him in the care of the vet to see if there was any hope of recovery.

What an empty house it now was!

How empty, drained, and lonely I felt.

I put on a good face to my friends and relatives, all of whom consoled me on hearing of the deaths of my cat and bird so close together.

It is times like these that test what you ultimately believe about life and reality, isn't it? The temptation to think that life is ultimately empty, meaningless, against you, full of tricks, not to be trusted, is strong when things go wrong. I found myself plagued with thoughts that I had become a dotty old woman, confused into believing that her cat and her parrot had been speaking to her.

Too much living on my own...losing my mind...
perhaps, even, there was an angry God out there,
now punishing me for questioning what I had been
taught to believe.

Pain, grief, and loneliness do that to you, don't
they? They readily take you out of your comfort
zone emotionally and mentally. You don't feel
right and you don't think right. You slip back
into old thought patterns. So I had to give myself
time to grieve. I kept telling myself to be easy on
myself.

It took some months—does it take longer as
you get older, or was that just me?—for the heavy
clouds on my mind to lift and for light and clear
thinking to return.

I came to believe that Faith's death was her way
of saying, "I have no more to say to you. Listen to
the universe and you will continue to hear what I
have been saying."

And why wouldn't I believe that Faith, too, was
somehow still with me after death, still part of the
universe and all it had to say to me?

I never thought Faith was comfortable with my or George's or the Christian idea of God, but I appreciated the way she helped me associate or connect God with the here and now and with all the universe rather than focus exclusively on God as over and above us all.

I now try to look and listen in ways that honor Faith's advice. I spend more time watching and appreciating TV documentaries about this planet and the universe. I delight in the magnitude of the universe, the development and beauty of this wonderful planet, and the varieties of life. Such programs help me to feel somehow more "at home" and more aware of God's presence.

And George? I wonder now whether George, left to himself, might have been able to speak on behalf of the universe the way Faith had. But George, the parrot, had been conditioned and could only repeat what he had heard. He never had an original thought of his own. However, George spoke for the Church and I respect my Church. George reminds me to hold on to my belief in God and Jesus, but

I have come to realize that my belief has become more expansive and inclusive than my Church seems willing to honor and proclaim—and far more than George was ever able to articulate.

In the time it took for me to deal with the deaths of Faith and George and recover some equilibrium, I felt myself pulled two ways. One way was to grief and loneliness. The other way was to deep gratitude for all the conversations we had. In the end, it was those discussions that helped me cope with their loss. And they are what sustain me now.

These days, I feel I am standing on firm ground, ready to face whatever life presents to me, and to face it with trust and inner security.

The **reality** of the **past**

I remember hearing, it must have been thirty or so years ago, someone saying that it's in midlife when you prepare yourself for old age. The speaker's advice was not to take unresolved issues into our later years or they will make life miserable for us.

I guess I remember the advice well because I have tried hard to act on it. I have tried to accept whatever had to be accepted, conscious of not wanting to take unresolved resentment into the years ahead. I have tried, especially, to forgive when forgiveness has been asked. I have also asked for forgiveness whenever I have been aware that I have hurt someone.

The speaker's advice would often come to mind in difficult times with the simple message to me, "Deal with it now. Resolve it. Come to some peace of mind about whatever it is."

It has been interesting and somewhat surprising, then, as I have reflected on my life since the conversations with Faith and George began, to find some memories of painful times resurfacing as I have tried to see God's presence in people and events.

It was not that I still had a lot of healing work to do on these painful episodes. Time certainly does some healing for a lot of hurts. No, it was more a matter of looking at them in the light of what I had come to appreciate about the universe and about God. Doing this has helped me arrive at a deeper and more contented sense of healing and resolution as the memories resurfaced.

Some of the significant issues that emerged for me were my father's temper and the atmosphere of fear it created in our home, my mother constantly showing favoritism to one of my sisters, bullying at school, friendships that ended unhappily, and the failure of my husband's dream work venture because of our accountant's dishonesty

As I reflected on these and other painful issues, my basic feeling was one of sadness that people so close to us in life hurt us—and we hurt others. How sad that we humans do not have the will to put an end to the cycle of intentional and unintentional pain we inflict on one another. I thought of my parents, both of whom probably had poor parenting and consequently parented us with flaws resulting from their own upbringing. I shudder to think what I might have passed on in my own parenting—but that's another story and we will come to that.

I don't want to excuse all bad behavior. No, my reflections had more to do with the human condition and its imperfections and of me letting go of an expectation that everyone, including myself and people closest to me, should never make mistakes or act out of their own personal weaknesses.

As I reflected on these events and people, I recalled Faith's advice to look at, listen to, and think about the universe.

So I spent time looking, listening, and thinking.

It eventually occurred to me that as I considered the universe, I was moved to look at a bigger picture, to look at life and existence more broadly. There was both invitation and challenge to consider existence in far greater scope than one individual life with its ups and downs. For example, it led me to ask, "Where will I be in a thousand million years' time?"

Have you ever thought of that?

A thousand million years! It is beyond imagining!

But it helped me to put things in a new perspective.

Perspective. That's what I have come to think ultimately helps healing and resolution.

I certainly needed to find both after the deaths of Elsie, Faith, and George.

My perspective now tries to bring what I know about the universe and what I believe about God together. Reflecting on the grandeur and the expansiveness of the universe and all its power and energy challenges me to be big-hearted. I want to be expansive like the universe, not small and petty and holding on to anything that has caused me pain. Similarly, reflecting on the mystery of God and on the message of Jesus challenges me not to get locked into my own small world.

When I think like this and recall my experiences of loving and being loved, of forgiving and of being forgiven, those experiences of love and forgiveness feel akin to the energy of the universe itself moving in me—something bigger than me. It's as though I'm being true to or giving expression to a basic movement of the universe itself.

So when I think of my parents now, and of other people who have ever hurt me, I try to get in touch with what I think of as a "universe movement," which I experience as a call to be expansive and big-hearted.

At the same time, I think of the mystery that God is—always everywhere, here, now. Thinking of this mystery challenges me to make the most of this human existence, to be grateful, to be the best I can with all my limitations as I give human expression to this mystery.

I think of my experiences of love and forgiveness and I am beginning to know, I mean really know deep inside me, what it means to say that to live in love is to experience the mystery of God here with us in this life.

When I turned the focus on myself and my actions I found it harder to come to self-acceptance and self-forgiveness. Why do we have such trouble with doing this?

When I think of my own mistakes and wrongdoing, I try to keep in mind what I was told many years ago, when I sought help and advice about something I did that greatly hurt a friend. I had not meant to hurt her. I just acted impulsively, interfered where I should not have, and made a bad situation even worse. I felt such guilt about that. I could not forgive my stupidity, my reckless and thoughtless behavior that caused great pain to my friend. Even when she said she forgave me, I continued to rage inwardly at myself.

When I sought help to deal with my anger and my lack of peace, I was helped by being directed to consider the difference between feelings of guilt and feelings of regret. I was asked whether I had deliberately intended to hurt my friend.

"No, no," I replied. "It was just unthinking foolishness. I would never want to hurt her."

"So you regret what you did?" I was asked.

I said an emphatic "Yes!" to that.

I was then asked to consider how close the feelings of regret and guilt are to each other and how often we confuse them. Often enough, we carry guilt and condemn ourselves over something we did or did not do as if we intended to cause hurt to someone when in reality we meant no harm. It is more a case of acknowledging we are not perfect human beings. We don't always have our act together. We make silly mistakes, to be regretted, but not to feel guilty about. We need to keep our feelings of guilt for intentional wrongdoing.

I put this among the best advice I have been given in my life. It helped me enormously when I realized I could regret what had happened, learn from the experience, and not beat myself with endless mea culpas as if I were a really bad person.

This difference between regret and guilt has been important for me to hold on to as I consider the mistakes of my own parenting. While I can regret the mistakes I made as a parent, I have stopped feeling the guilt I carried for many years about them. I never intended to hurt my children in any way.

We are so quick to berate ourselves because we make mistakes, aren't we? Who of us ever willfully intended to fail in any significant aspect of being mother or father? Yet, how many of us made mistakes, some of which are probably embedded in our children?

When it comes to actions of mine for which I should and do feel guilt, I want my genuine sorrow to lead me to forgive myself as readily as I forgive others who ask for my forgiveness. More than that, I want to do something about it if I can, which is why in the past year or so some people have received a letter from me asking their forgiveness for a wrong or a hurt I did them.

"To be on earth the heart of God" comes readily to me now. The conviction is deeper and stronger than earlier because it embraces the good and the not so good in my life. It invites me to let go, to move on, to stop hoarding or holding on, to let life, love, forgiveness, spirit, God, universe flow on in me. Not block it. That's the challenge.

And to think it was my cat who led me to this understanding!

Imagine that!

The reality of
the present
and **the future**

I'm coming to the conclusion that growing older has a lot going for it, though I suspect some people might think it's easy for me to say that. I enjoy reasonably good health and my doctor tells me my heart is likely to keep on pumping for years yet. I live comfortably, my mind still operates with clarity, and I have frequent contact with my wonderful family.

I know some people experience later life very differently. I see evidence of it here in this retirement community. I know several people here who are hanging on to life by a thread, all the while wishing it were ended. Some other people here still have a strong hold on life but are physically incapacitated or have memory loss or suffer acute anxiety or some other significant ailment. I realize this can be the reality of getting older, but I do not want it to cast a heavy cloud over my own life, as if that is inevitably what is waiting for all of us.

Most people in this community do not live with undue apprehension or walk around with fear-glazed looks. Whenever my family and friends ask me what it is like here, I find myself talking about openness and confidence. You might be surprised at "confidence," but that is what strikes me. Most of the people here carry a sense of a life well lived and worth living. They're not just about waiting for death to come. They believe, and are helped by the staff here to believe, that this is a stage of life to be lived to the fullest.

I like that. I am glad I am not surrounded by people who think life is all downhill once you retire or reach your seventies.

That has been one of the best learning experiences for me about aging: to mix with people

who think positively. I recommend it wholeheart-
edly. It must be part of a good recipe for life at all
stages.

I try to be involved in activities that keep my
mind and my body active. I've found my new interest in the universe and this planet has been a wonderful boon. Who could have predicted my mind
and knowledge would expand so much in these
years of my life? I certainly didn't! I had presumed
my mind would gradually wind down. Now I'm
learning all sorts of things.

I smile when I hear Church people suggest "you
should not disturb the faith of older folk." I think
we older people have a capacity for wisdom and
expansiveness that far exceeds that of our midlife
years. I know for myself that in those mid-years of
my life I was very much locked into seeing reality
and "truth" from the narrow perspective of a mid-
dle-class, Church-abiding, white woman. I had no
reason to question what I had been taught about
life and meaning and God. I suspect if I'd heard
anyone talk then about what I now believe about

life, meaning, and God, I would have bristled and refused to listen.

Yes, age does have its advantages—if we are open and want to keep learning.

At times, I catch myself wondering whether I am pessimistic or optimistic about the future of humanity.

There is much to make me despair. For example, I can easily despair when I think about supposedly Christian political leaders being persuaded more by party politics, personal gain, and the ear of lobbyists than the gospel message to *be* neighbor and to work for the common good. And it is not only politicians. I shudder when I think of many Christians accepting so readily a message of a heavenly God rewarding "good" people with material benefits. I doubt whether Jesus would be happy with the level of elitism, greed, and division or with the injustice and poverty in much of our world.

What gives me hope is to see a younger generation far more concerned about the environment and social justice and being world citizens than my generation ever was. I think some young people are already working to dismantle the religious, social, political, and economic barriers and divisions they inherited. I hope they know there are older people like me cheering them on. I believe they are living a message that the universe is calling all of us to hear: Stop the violence; end the divisions; *be* neighbor; care for the planet that nurtured us into existence.

As for myself in the years left to me, I intend to live life as fully as I can, but I also have to be realistic about it. The years ahead will not be without their trials, I'm sure. I expect that. I hope that whatever limitations or afflictions come my way, I may be able to face them with acceptance and equanimity.

I've learned that the likelihood of getting Alzheimer's increases significantly after the age of eighty. If anything does not seem fair about the human condition, this devastating disease must be near the top of the list. I find myself asking: What does my present understanding of God and God at work in the universe say about Alzheimer's disease or any other debilitating condition?

I can only say I do not believe God "permits," or worse, "sends" such afflictions. That would be a cruel God for sure.

I see disease as part and parcel of human existence, where things do not always work as we would like them to. Our human task is to work with our God-given gifts and abilities and increasing knowledge to reduce the incidence and effect of diseases. We have done so very effectively with some.

One day there may be a cure for Alzheimer's. If I should be afflicted before the cure comes, I can only hope that good care, the sort I see here in this community, will ensure life is as dignified and peaceful as possible for me. God *is* here after all.

Further ahead for me is the reality of death. This gets me thinking of caterpillars and butterflies.

I cannot imagine that a caterpillar looks at a butterfly and says to itself, "That'll be me, someday."

I face my death mindful of life ending but trusting also that I will be transformed and will emerge into a way of existence totally beyond my human imagination—just as a caterpillar can have no idea of what lies ahead of it when it ceases to exist as a caterpillar.

I believe that death will not be the end of me. I will "live on" in ways unknown to me.

I hope that the insights I have come to about the universe, God, religion, life, and expansiveness will "live on" in my children and grandchildren and in generations to come. That hope has led me to share my story in these pages. However, I suspect they will be enlightened in their own ways as God and the universe unfold in their lives. They just have to listen and be attentive.

I approach the years ahead of me with a deep appreciation for the gift of life in this beautiful world and for the wonderful privilege of being aware of its beauty. I am so grateful that I finally learned how connected I am with this world, this universe, with God, and with all that is.

I believe my human way of being "the heart of God on earth" will give way to being *in* the heart of God for billions and billions of years—and beyond.

Imagine *that*!

Easter: Living on

I wasn't too sure what title to give this last chapter. I've said I wanted to write something especially for my children and their children and their children and their children. However, it is not so much that I want them to keep on remembering me after I have died. It's more that I want them to know in the depths of their being, that their deceased brothers and sisters, mothers and fathers, grandmothers and grandfathers, great-grandmothers and great-grandfathers—all the way back along the line of their forebears—are with them as an integral part of who they are.

I want them to know that what we hear as "the communion of saints" is not really about a community of deceased people overlooking us from some place way above us. No, this communion is part and parcel of who we are and our connection with the mystery of God and all that exists.

I think of Easter and the great news it is for Christians. I know Christians basically celebrate Easter in terms of Jesus being raised by God and being taken up into heaven. But in light of all I have shared in these pages, Easter has taken on a new meaning for me, one that is faithful to the gospel stories about people meeting Jesus after he had died: *He is still here with you.*

The followers of Jesus clearly had a strong sense of that and it sustained them. They believed the spirit of God that gave life and insight to Jesus was with and in them. They were to live knowing Jesus was somehow still with them. That is a wonderful Easter message for us today also. Christian faith invites us to believe that the Spirit in Jesus "lives on" in us as we keep his story, his message, and his spirit alive. It invites us to believe there is a power and a presence in us that can do far more than we dare ask or imagine.

We are all part of this Easter story. The story invites us to believe that we too will "live on" and will be present to those who come after us.

"Know that I am always with you," says Jesus at the end of Matthew's gospel.

My family, know that I am always with you.

Keep on imagining and believing that!

Afterword

Living on in ways unknown:
Mary Janet Morwood

Although Mary Janet Morwood did not physically write or dictate this book, and was not alive when the writing began, I had considered naming her as the author.

I wanted the book to bear her name because all the writing was done with attentiveness to her spirit, present and living on in one of her descendants. This seems akin to the contemporary understanding of how "revelation" in Scripture works.

God did not dictate the words but worked through the minds and hearts of people attuned to the activity of the Divine Presence in human affairs. As such, the Bible is recognized by Christians as "God's book."

This book is the product of Mary's spirit very much living on in my heart and mind. It *is* "Mary Morwood's book."

Mary Janet Edgar married Jack Joseph Harvey Morwood and gave birth to twelve children: Alan, Patricia, Kevin, Marie, Peter, Desmond, Joan, Noel, Ian, Francis, Carmel, and Michael.

She died at age thirty-six.

Mary lives on in her children, her grandchildren, her great-grandchildren and her great-great-grandchildren. She lives on in ways she and her children could never have imagined—and in innumerable ways that her descendants may never be able to pinpoint.

In wanting to use Mary Morwood as author, my intent was to draw attention to, acknowledge, and celebrate what is true for every one of us. First, whoever we are, we are in communion with whoever has gone before us, with whoever has enlivened and loved us—and if those people have died, they are still with us in spirit and will always be part of us. They will continue to influence us in ways we may never be fully conscious of.

Second, what is true of those who have died and of their continued influence on us is, and always will be, true of ourselves. Whether we have children or not, our lives have touched others in ways we will never fully appreciate because we will never fully know. The ripples of influence have already spread way, way beyond anything we could imagine, starting perhaps with just a smile we gave a stranger in a supermarket one day or the help we gave a friend.

While practical considerations worked against naming Mary Morwood as author, I believe she and all our deceased relatives and friends invite us to marvel at a "communion of saints" and the ways lives touch and will keep on touching in ways beyond human imagination.

Also by **Michael Morwood**

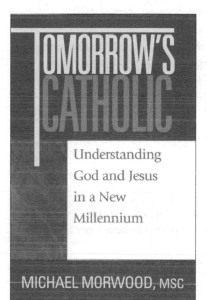

TOMORROW'S CATHOLIC

Understanding
God and Jesus
in a New
Millennium

MICHAEL MORWOOD, MSC

160 pages • $12.95 • order 227243

Order today!

Call **1-800-321-0411**
or visit us on the web at
www.23rdpublications.com

In clear, down-to-earth language, this book tries to bridge the gap between church doctrine and the essential gospel message that is our Christian legacy. It offers a fascinating outline of contemporary cosmology that connects the message of Jesus and the world we live in today. The suggested questions for discussion, the extensive bibliography, and comprehensive index make this a valuable adult faith development resource.

TWENTY
THIRD *23rd*

More **GREAT** spirituality titles

God's Tender Mercy *Reflections on Forgiveness*
JOAN CHITTISTER

Sr. Joan Chittister tackles the virtue of mercy and its connection to forgiveness. She challenges us to stop judging, accusing, and criticizing those we label "sinners" and to be realistic about our actions before we "throw that first stone." This challenging and inspiring book is spiritual reading at its very best.

Hardcover • 80 pages • $10.95 • order 957996

Beyond Pain *Job, Jesus, and Joy*
MAUREEN PRATT

This is an in-depth look at how people can live with pain, and even come to see it with the eyes of faith. It is for all who live with deep, life-altering pain and want to have more joy, faith, and purpose in their lives.

168 pages • $14.95 • order 957866

The Breath of the Soul *Reflections on Prayer*
JOAN CHITTISTER

These soul-searing reflections touch the heart and mind and challenge readers to see prayer as the way to touch God in all that they do. This is great spiritual reading for all who long for prayer to be at the core of their lives.

Hardcover • 144 pages • $12.95 • order 957477

1-800-321-0411 • www.23rdpublications.com